A MAGIC CIRCLE BOOK

JOEY'S SECRET

written by **BLAIR McCRACKEN**
illustrated by **JOEL SNYDER**

THEODORE CLYMER
SENIOR AUTHOR, READING 360

GINN AND COMPANY
A XEROX EDUCATION COMPANY

Library of Congress Catalog Card Number: 72-77625

International Standard Book Number: 0–663–25490–6

Joey Perez was the best climber in the neighborhood and he knew it. He liked to climb more than he liked to do anything else. Looking down on backyards made him feel that the whole world belonged to him.

Joey's room opened onto a fire escape. From there he could climb up or he could jump over to the porch roof next door and climb down to Mr. Lee's laundry on the first floor. By crossing along the roof, he could reach the fire escape in back of the glass factory and watch Mr. Collins cut glass. There were so many ways Joey could go. He still hadn't tried them all.

Joey's family had lived in the neighborhood only three weeks. His father looked after the apartment house where they lived.

People had been cross about the climbing in the last place they had lived, and Joey's parents had been angry with him. Joey's dad had told him he would use the belt if he didn't stop climbing.

Joey took the chance and climbed anyway. That's how he had met so many grown-ups. Besides Mr. Lee and Mr. Collins, he knew old Mrs. Olsen and her four cats, and he had seen Mr. Schwartz riding his exercise machine. Sometimes he even went as far as Mr. Canotti's store and climbed down to get some day-old doughnuts.

Today, the last day of summer vacation, Joey had jumped over to the porch roof next door and crawled across it. As he stretched over to reach the roof of the glass factory, he slipped. Quickly he grabbed hold of a drain pipe to keep himself from falling to the ground. Then he swung back over to the porch roof and to safety — with very sore hands.

While he sat on the roof waiting for his hands to stop hurting, he heard a noise above him and looked up.

"What are you doing there?" asked a voice. The voice belonged to a freckle-faced girl with the reddest hair Joey had ever seen. She was leaning out of a third-floor window of the building Joey lived in and she was smiling.

"I'm just sitting and looking," said Joey.

"Hey, don't you live in my building?" the girl asked.

"I guess so," answered Joey.

"Boy, you're not very friendly," the girl said. "What are you looking at?"

Joey smiled. "I can see everything," he boasted. "All the way down to the end of the block. And I know everybody who lives there too!"

The girl pulled her head inside the window. "I'd be afraid to go up there!" she called. "Why don't you come out front?"

Joey climbed down the fire escape and swung in through the back window to his room. No one was at home, so he headed for the front steps.

On his way through the hall, Joey spotted a box. It was one of the boxes his dad had brought down for the clean-up men. In the box on top of newspapers and cans was a toy airplane. The propeller was missing and the tail hung down. "I can fix that," thought Joey. "I've got just the thing." He took the key from around his neck and unlocked the door to the apartment.

He ran into his room and poked through some things in a shoe box by the bed. Finally, he found an old ice-cream stick. He put the stick on the plane with the help of a rubber band. Then he found some glue in a box near the stove and stuck the tail together.

"I'll leave it here to dry," he thought. "It'll be good for Luis to play with." He put the plane on the table and ran into the hall.

When he got outside, he found Luis drawing on the steps with some purple chalk.

"Don't do that!" Joey said. "We just cleaned up these steps!"

"I told him that, but he wouldn't listen!"

Joey looked up and saw the girl with the red hair.

"What's your name?" she asked.

"Joey Perez," he answered.

"My name is Lucinda Scott. Are you going to school tomorrow?"

"Yeah," said Joey. "Are you?"

"Yes. It's not bad. We're getting a good teacher this year." Lucinda began to bounce a ball against the building.

Joey walked off to Mr. Canotti's store with Luis trailing along behind him.

The next day Joey arrived early at his new school. The sun was hot, and for once Joey was glad that he wasn't playing ball.

Some boys were trading cards. One boy even traded a brand-new model car for a football card. Joey wished he had something to trade.

That evening Joey sat on the front steps. His mother had gone to the laundry and he was watching Luis. Earlier, while he was helping his father clean the basement, Joey had found a spy car in a box of trash. The top didn't flip open the way it should, but Joey thought he could use a little piece of wire to pull it back and make it work again. He was bending the wire when Lucinda came out onto the steps with a boy about Joey's age.

"This is Peter," Lucinda said.

"That's a cool spy car," Peter said. "Where did you get it?"

Joey didn't want to say that he had found it in the trash, so he just explained that he was fixing it. He showed them how he was twisting the wire underneath. Peter looked at the car for a moment and then asked Joey if he wanted to play stickball.

"Go ahead," said Lucinda. "I'll watch Luis."

"Thanks," Joey called as he ran over to the other boys.

During the stickball game the boys asked Joey to bring something to school to trade. So the next morning he took the plane he had fixed. When Peter saw the plane, he asked Joey if he could look at it.

"It really works," Joey said, handing it to him.

Peter twisted the propeller around and let it go. "You're right!" he exclaimed.

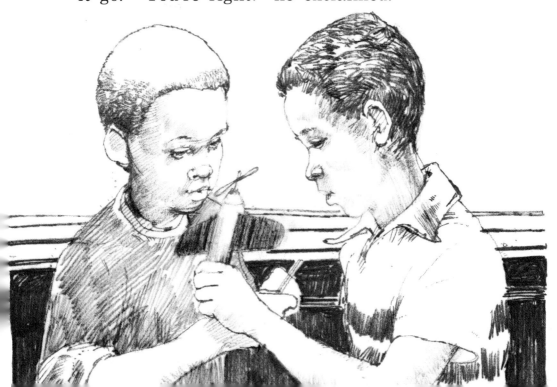

A boy named Lew West came running over. "Can I try it too?" he asked.

Joey was afraid the plane would break again, but he said, "O.K."

After trying the plane, Lew asked if Joey would trade it for a set of ten monster cards. Joey thought for a minute and agreed to the trade.

From then on, the boys asked him to play
ball all the time. He played before school,
during recess, and then after supper until
dark. Joey was too busy playing ball to climb
much anymore.

One day Lucinda was sitting on the steps with Luis, watching the boys play ball. Luis was playing with a rusty can that he had picked up. Lucinda had tried many times to get him to give it up. She finally called to Joey, "Your brother needs something to play with."

Joey ran over when the boys were resting. He took the spy car out of his pocket and gave it to Luis.

"Be careful!" he warned his little brother. "I fixed it, but it isn't very strong." Luis smiled and began to run the car back and forth on the steps.

A little while later Walt came out of the apartment building. He was a bigger boy who lived upstairs. Every now and then he stopped to play ball, but most of the time he went off with some friends.

"Where did you get that car, kid?" he asked. "That's my brother's car."

Luis looked up and stopped playing. "It is not," he said. "Joey gave it to me."

"Who's Joey?" Walt asked.

Luis pointed down the street. "He's my brother!" Luis said. "He's over there."

Walt yelled and Joey came running. As soon as Joey got to the steps, he could tell something was wrong.

"Where did you get that car?" Walt asked, pointing to Luis.

Joey's brother was holding the car behind his back and his eyes were filling with tears.

"What do you mean? I just found it," said Joey.

"I don't think you found it," said Walt. "I think you took it. You live here, don't you?"

"Yeah," said Joey. "So what?"

"So you could have taken it!"

"I don't know what you're talking about," said Joey. He looked straight at Walt. "I found it and it's mine."

By this time all the other boys had come over. They stood around listening. Most of them were afraid of Walt. He was in the sixth grade, so they listened to what he said.

"He's been trading some other stuff too!" said one of the boys.

"I'd like to know where he gets it," said Walt. "His father works here. I've seen this kid climbing on the fire escape out back. Anyone who lives in this building had better watch out for his stuff."

Joey was so angry he felt cold and shaky inside. He knew the car was his. He just didn't want to say he had found it in the trash. It was hard enough being the superintendent's son without telling them he got his toys in the garbage. He stared at the sidewalk and kicked the edge of the step with his sneaker.

One of the boys pointed at Lew who was holding Joey's plane. "What about the plane?" he asked loudly. "Lew gave him a good set of monster cards for it!"

"Let me see that!" said Walt. He turned the plane over and over in his hands. "Yeah, that belongs to my brother too!" he said, looking angrily at Joey.

"This guy is some thief!" said one of the boys. "I saw him on that fire escape the other day before school. He better stay away from our place!"

Most of the boys were standing in back of Walt by this time. Only Luis stood by Joey. Lucinda just sat on the steps and watched.

"How do you know that car belongs to your brother?" asked one of the younger boys.

"Because the fender was off the back and the top was broken," said Walt. "He's been looking for it, and now I know where it is!" He reached out and grabbed it away from Luis.

"Hey!" said Joey. "Cut that out!" Walt just walked away grinning, holding both toys in his hand.

Joey started to run after him. But the other boys stood in his way, and one of them shoved him back against the steps. When Joey fought back, some of the boys grabbed his arms.

"They're mine!" he yelled, whirling on them. "I'm telling you they are!"

Lucinda said quietly, "Maybe they are, you guys. Anyway, how come Walt knows so much about his brother's stuff?"

But the boys turned and walked away without answering. Joey just stood there. He wanted to cry, but not in front of Lucinda and his little brother. He ran into the house, through the hall, and out into the backyard. Swinging himself up on the first rung of the fire escape, he climbed quickly to the roof. He took a deep breath and pulled himself up over the edge.

The sun was hot, and the tar had a bitter smell. The yard below with its broken fence looked far away. If Joey looked to the right of the tree next door, he could see the pigeons circling over the cage on Mr. Schwartz's roof. He wished he were like the pigeons and could fly up into the sky and disappear.

The next day at school, no one spoke to Joey. When the boys saw him coming onto the playground at recess, they walked away. Joey decided not to follow them. He stood by the door and frowned at his shadow on the sidewalk, knowing that they were looking at him as they talked. Lucinda came over and stood beside him. He didn't look up.

"Why don't you tell them where you got it?" she asked.

"Because it's none of their business," Joey said crossly.

"Well, it is, kind of," said Lucinda. "They don't know you."

"Forget it," said Joey.

That night as Joey's mother was clearing away the supper dishes, there was a knock on the door. Mr. Perez opened the door to find Walt's mother, Mrs. Hodges, standing in the hall. She seemed very angry.

"I just came down to tell you that you had better keep an eye on that boy of yours!" she said in a loud voice.

"What do you mean?" asked Mr. Perez. His wife came to stand beside him, still holding a dish in her hands. Joey backed into his room. His heart was pounding loudly.

"My boys told me about his stealing their toys. He climbs around on that fire escape like a thief!"

"He's climbing again?" Mr. Perez asked.

"So you know about all that, do you? Well, your kid had better watch himself!" Mrs. Hodges turned and walked away. "I have a good mind to tell the police. . . ."

Her voice got farther and farther away as she went up the stairs. She didn't stop talking until she was back in her apartment and had closed the door.

When it was quiet again, Mr. Perez closed the door and turned around.

"Joey," he said quietly but firmly. "I told you not to climb."

Joey's mother looked as if she was going to cry. She quickly went into the kitchen.

Joey knew that when his father used his quiet voice, he was very angry. He knew that his father was going to hit him with the belt that was hanging on the closet door. He tried to tell his father that everyone had made a mistake. But his father would not listen. All Mr. Perez cared about was that Joey had made Mrs. Hodges very angry. Mrs. Hodges was a tenant. And an angry tenant could cause trouble for a superintendent. Joey had put his whole family in danger by making Mrs. Hodges angry.

At school the next day, Joey moved very stiffly. Everyone in the class knew what had happened. Some of the boys had heard Joey crying, and Walt had told everyone what his mother had said to Mr. Perez. Each time Mrs. Portmann, their teacher, looked up, someone was whispering or giggling. They all seemed to be looking at Joey.

After a while Joey put his head down on his desk as if he were very tired. Mrs. Portmann went over to ask him what was the matter, but Joey would not raise his head from his arms.

One of the boys giggled. "Better watch out. He might take your pencil!"

"Just what is going on?" Mrs. Portmann asked, looking sternly at the boys who were smiling.

"Uh — he just got what he deserved," one of them answered. "His father found out he was helping himself to everybody's stuff."

Mrs. Portmann looked down at Joey again and saw him clench his fist on the desk. Joey kept his head down.

"All right, boys. That's enough," she said. "Everyone get back to work."

When the recess bell rang, Mrs. Portmann asked Joey to stay in the classroom. He was sure the teacher was going to punish him.

After all the children had left and the room was very quiet, Mrs. Portmann sat down on the desk next to Joey's. She didn't say anything at first, but when she saw that Joey was not going to look at her, she began talking to him very gently.

"Joey," she said, "I can tell that something is very wrong. Is there anything I can do to help you? I'm sure that if we talk it over, together we can figure out a way to set things straight again."

Joey did not feel like talking. But he finally raised his head after Mrs. Portmann told him that she trusted him and that she understood how sometimes things get mixed up. He still wouldn't look at her, but he told her a little bit of what had happened.

Mrs. Portmann was able to guess the rest. She seemed to know how he felt. She said that she might know a way to work things out if he could just hang on a little while longer. Joey said he thought he could.

The days that followed were hard ones for Joey. It wouldn't have been so bad if he hadn't been playing ball with the boys before. Since he had, it was hard to stand by the side of the building and watch. Most of the time he just stayed inside, no matter how hot it was. He closed the door of his room and sat on the edge of the bed reading the same comic books again and again. He didn't even climb on the fire escape, because of what the boys had said about his climbing into other people's apartments.

After a while Joey noticed that when he passed Lucinda, she would never stop to talk. Joey felt that he had no friends. Even Lucinda believed what the boys were saying and she, too, had decided he was a thief.

Then one afternoon Mrs. Portmann paid Walt's mother a visit. She knew Mrs. Hodges quite well because Walt had been in her class when he was in third grade. Mrs. Portmann told Mrs. Hodges that Joey had found the toys in boxes of trash and had fixed them up for his little brother to play with. But Mrs. Hodges didn't believe a word of it. She said she knew that Joey was a "little criminal," and that her sons had told her all about Joey climbing on the fire escape when he thought no one was looking.

While they were talking, Walt came in to leave his school books before he went out to play. He was surprised to find Mrs. Portmann there. After they said hello, Mrs. Portmann asked Walt to show her the toys that everyone was making a fuss about. At first Walt said he didn't know where they were. Finally he brought them out and held them up for Mrs. Portmann to see.

"Are those the things you've been talking about?" cried Walt's mother. "Why I threw them out ages ago when I cleaned out your room!"

Suddenly her face grew very red. She realized that what Mrs. Portmann had been telling her about Joey was true. Joey had never stolen anything. He had only found some broken toys that she had thrown out without telling her sons.

A few minutes later a strange group made its way down the stairs to the Perez's apartment. First came Mrs. Hodges, looking very embarrassed. Then clumping along in back of her came Walt, looking very cross. Last of all came Mrs. Portmann, smiling to herself and looking very pleased.

When Joey opened the door, both he and his parents were surprised. Joey was frightened and began to back away.

Mrs. Hodges apologized to Mr. and Mrs. Perez. Then Walt mumbled something about making a mistake. Then only Mrs. Portmann was left standing in the hall. She smiled at Joey and began to explain the whole thing to his father and mother.

Mrs. Perez began to smile and then she laughed. Mr. Perez looked pleased, too, and ruffled Joey's hair. Mrs. Perez thanked Mrs. Portmann for all the trouble she had gone to for Joey's sake. Mr. Perez told Joey to stay out of the trash from now on and to stay out of trouble too. But Joey could tell that everyone was really very pleased to find out the truth.

Joey was happiest of all. He thanked his teacher and promised to work extra hard on his math. Suddenly he felt so full of happiness that he couldn't stay inside. The grown-ups were still talking as he slipped into the hall.

There was Lucinda standing on the stairs, trying to look as though she hadn't been listening. Joey just looked at her and walked right out to the front steps. When she came out behind him, he didn't turn around. Lucinda sat down on the top step.

"That's nice, they got it straight, Joey," she said quietly.

"Yeah," he said.

When she held out a piece of grape gum, he took it.

The next day Joey was feeling so good that he ran almost all the way home after school. Luis could hardly keep up with him. Word had gotten around fast. By the end of recess everyone had been so nice to him that he hadn't known what to think. Some of the boys had even asked him to play ball after school.

But Joey's pride was hurt, and he hadn't said Yes right away. It would have sounded as though he were willing to take whatever they gave out. He had mumbled something about having to work. But he hadn't been able to keep the joy from showing in his eyes.

His mother had asked him to pick up some milk on his way home, so he stopped at Mr. Canotti's store on the corner. He was standing by the door letting Luis count the different prizes in the gum machine, when Mr. Canotti called to him.

"Hey, Joey. How about carrying some of those boxes outside for me? I could use a hand around here!"

By the time Mr. Canotti had the milk in a bag, Joey had stacked all the boxes neatly outside.

"That was fast," Mr. Canotti said. "Listen, Joey. How would you like a job after school? I need someone to do that for me every day. You can earn yourself a little money."

Joey could hardly believe his ears. No more fixing up old toys! He would be able to buy new ones. He was so excited he felt like jumping up and down. But instead, he shook Mr. Canotti's hand and said, "That would be O.K., Mr. Canotti. I'd like to. I'll be here tomorrow after school!"

As they walked home, Luis looked at Joey and said, "Once Mr. Canotti finds out how good you are at fixing things, I bet he'll have more jobs for you!"

"I hope so!" said Joey.

After supper that night, Joey climbed out the window of his room onto the fire escape. It was the first time in a long while. The night air was soft and warm against his face. He felt so happy inside, it was as if he were a balloon about to burst. In the dim light he looked across the yard to Mrs. Olsen's window. She was putting out the food for her cats and talking to them softly. Mr. Schwartz had his window wide open, and he was riding slowly on his exercise machine. Everything seemed just right. Joey sat for a moment, listening to the sounds of people's voices drifting up from below and enjoying the hot, toasted smell that rose from the laundry.

Then, as it grew darker, Joey climbed up to the roof — his roof. A few stars began to show in the sky. He could still hear the voices of the boys playing ball on the street below. Happily he leaned back against a corner in the darkness. "I'll play with them tomorrow," he thought. "After work."

ABCDEFGHIJK 765432
PRINTED IN THE UNITED STATES OF AMERICA